*For Alistair*
~J.S.

*For Katie*
~ C.W.

*Reprinted 1997*

First published in 1996 by Magi Publications
22 Manchester Street, London W1M 5PG

This edition published 1997

Text © 1996 Julie Sykes
Illustrations © 1996 Catherine Walters

Printed in Belgium by Proost NV, Turnhout

ISBN  1 85430 436 4

# Hide and Narrow Squeak

*by* Julie Sykes

*illustrated by* Catherine Walters

In a large burrow in Teasel Wood lived Rolly
Rabbit and his family.

One day, Rolly's mother interrupted his
afternoon nap to tell him she was going out.

"Rolly, look after the little ones for me," she said.
And before he could say "Buck's your uncle",
she had hopped away into the bright sunshine.

Rolly looked at the little ones, roughly tumbling
over each other in the grass.
"Come on, little ones," said Rolly. "We're going
to play a game."

"But we're already playing a game!" cried a little
one in surprise.
"This is a nice game with no rough stuff," said Rolly.
"It's called Hide and Seek."

"We don't know how to play it," the little ones
exclaimed.

"I close my eyes and count to ten, while you run
away to hide. Then I have to find you," said Rolly.
The little ones didn't think it sounded much fun.

"No biting? No kicking or pushing?"

"Absolutely not! I'll start counting now.
One, two, three . . . "

By the time Rolly had reached ten, all the little ones had disappeared.

"Ready or not, I'm coming!" called Rolly,
and hopped towards the trees.

Sticking out from behind an oak
tree was the tip of a tail.
Ah, a little one!
Rolly sneaked towards the tail
and gave it a nip.

"Ouch!" yelled Barny Badger grumpily.
"Go and pull your own tail!"
"Sorry," mumbled Rolly. "I'm playing
a game with the little ones."

Rolly scampered off to the edge of the
cornfield where it was nice and peaceful.
But wait! What was that rustling sound?
Rolly pounced.

"Eek!" squealed Merry Mouse, and she bit Rolly
on the nose. "You thundering bully! You've
flattened my nest!"
"Sorry," said Rolly again. "I thought you were
a little one."
"I *am* a little one," snapped Merry crossly.

Rolly hopped on into the wood.
By the side of the path was a hollow log.
It appeared to be snoring.
"It *must* be the little ones this time," thought Rolly.
"Boo!" he shouted.

"Oh, you've woken me up!" said an angry voice,
and Wiz Weasel poked his head out from the
hollow trunk. "Go away, you rowdy rabbit!"
"I'm sorry. I thought you were a little
one, too," said Rolly unhappily.

"This game isn't as much fun as I thought,"
Rolly muttered to himself as he bounded along.
"Where *are* the little ones? I hope I haven't
lost them." Suddenly he spotted something hidden
in a nearby bramble bush. Rolly hopped closer.
Deep in the undergrowth he could see a speck of
fur and a pointed ear.
"Got them!" cried Rolly, and he tweaked the ear.

"Yap!" cried a little voice, and
"Grr!" a deeper voice answered, as a fox
leapt out of the bush to defend her cub.
Rolly didn't wait to say sorry this time.
He sprang away and ran for cover,
as fast as his paws would carry him.

The fox ran after him, gnashing her teeth.
Rolly was scared.
The fox would eat him if she caught him.
*Then* who would look after the little ones?
Rolly came to his burrow . . .

. . . and dived down it.

Just in time!

The fox was behind him, growling and snarling.

SNAP! She missed him by a whisker.

That was a narrow squeak!

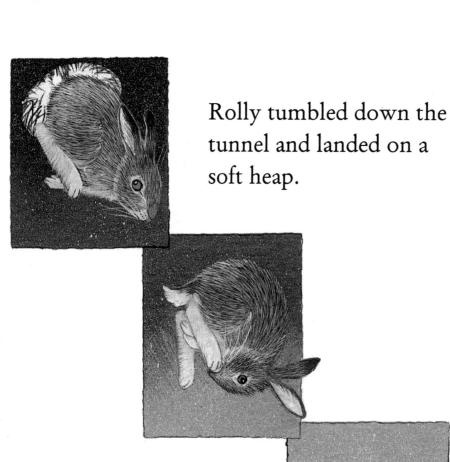

Rolly tumbled down the
tunnel and landed on a
soft heap.

It was the little ones,
all curled up together.

"Where have you been?" asked one of them.
"We've been here for ages."
"Hiding together was *such* fun," said another,
sitting up. "Can we play it again?"
Rolly thought about his narrow escape, and
shook his head. "Mother will be back soon.
But I'll tell you a story instead . . ."

Excitedly, all the little ones gathered
round him.
"What's the story called?" they asked.
Rolly thought about the fox and
her snapping teeth.
*"Hide and Narrow Squeak!"*
he said.